LET'S COUNT GOATS!

FOR THEO
—M. F.

FOR CHARLIE
—J. T.

ISBN 978-0-545-51110-0

Text copyright © 2010 by Mem Fox.
Illustrations copyright © 2010 by Jan Thomas.
All rights reserved. Published by Scholastic Inc.,
557 Broadway, New York, NY 10012,
by arrangement with Simon & Schuster Books for Young Readers,
an imprint of Simon & Schuster Children's Publishing Division.
SCHOLASTIC and associated logos are trademarks and/or
registered trademarks of Scholastic Inc.

12 11 10 9 8 7 6 5 4 3 2   14 15 16 17/0

Printed in the U.S.A.   40

First Scholastic printing, October 2012

Book design by Lauren Rille
The text for this book is set in Grenadine.
The illustrations for this book are rendered digitally.

LET'S COUNT GOATS!

words by
Mem Fox

goats by
Jan Thomas

SCHOLASTIC INC.

Here we see a mountain goat frisking in the sun.

And here we see a city goat going for a run.

But can we count the **SEASIDE** goats?
(I think there's only one.)

Here we see
a drinking goat.

And here a goat is eating.

But can we count
the **LITTLE** goats,
lost and loudly bleating?

Here we see an airport goat
looking for her cases.

But can we count the **PILOT** goats with goggles on their faces?

Here we see a show-off goat playing on the bars.

But can we count the **ROWDY** goats careering round in cars?

Here we see an over goat.

And this one's going under.

Here we see a sandpit goat playing with his toys.

But can we count
the **TRUMPET** goats
making all the noise?

Here we see a summer goat
with nothing left to mow.

But can we count
the **WINTER** goats
huddled in the snow?

Here we see a fireman goat climbing through the smoke.

But can we count the **RESCUED**

goats trying not to choke?

Here we see a soccer goat roaring at the ref!

But can we count the **CHEERING** goats who must be going deaf?

Here we see the story goats
and all their shining eyes.

Now . . .

can you count
their pricked-up ears?

You can?

I'm not surprised!